There's something very simple that
I need you to remember.

When I say

OOH

you say

AAH

as loudly as you can.

Are you ready?

OOH

I can't hear you.

OOH

One more time, *even louder.*

OOH

That's it.

Now, if you see the colour

RED

pat your

HEAD

OOH OOH OOH OOH OOH OOH OOH OOH OOH OOH OOH

STOP hitting your head. It sounds like it *hurts*.

OK, there's one more thing.
When you see an

ANT

you say

UNDER-
PANTS

I beg your pardon, that's a bit

RUDE!

Now you're just being

silly!

Well, I need you to be nice,
because I'd like you to meet my friend.

This is my donkey.
He says "Hello".

His name is

OOH

What are you doing?
You've frightened

OOH

Oh no, he's running away.

Now he's hiding from you.

What's that on his nose?

Donkeys don't wear

UND
PAN

ER-
TS

TS

At least I don't think they do.

LOOK

he's coming back.
But he seems a little sad.

I think we should

speak really quietly

so we don't

scare him

again.

Can you do that?

Don't forget to whisper.

Is everything OK,

OOH?

He still looks sad.

I think he's lost something.

What do you think he's lost?

You're

being

silly

again!

I've already told you.

DONKEYS DON'T WEAR UNDER-PANTS

What else could he have lost?

OK
OK
OK

You
actually
think
donkeys
DO
wear
underpants.

So where do you think they are?

THEY'RE ON YOUR HEAD?

I can't see them.
Maybe we should look somewhere else.

While you're looking,
here's something else to remember.

If you see a

CLOUD

say your name out

LOUD

That's a lovely name.

OOH

says he's pleased to meet you.

HEE HAW

But he still can't find his underpants.
Now where could they be?

That's it,

OOH

Let's get to the bottom of this.

YAY!

He's found them.

I think he deserves a round of applause.

Hang on, he tells me they're not his.

So who do they belong to?

They're your

UND
PAN

ER-
TS?

You wear
pink frilly
underpants
with yellow
spots?

He actually thinks they look good on him.

OOH!

OK, there's one last thing I want you to do.

Every time I turn the

PAGE

you must

WAVE

Bye bye

OOH

It looks like donkeys really *do* wear underpants.

But only on their heads.

Yes, I know you said
they're your underpants,
but now they belong to

OOH

You can stop waving now, he's gone.